First published in Great Britain in September 2012 by Bloomsbury Publishing Plc
Published in the United States of America in October 2012
by Walker Publishing Company, Inc., a division of Bloomsbury Publishing, Inc.
www.bloomsburykids.com

For information about permission to reproduce selections from this book, write
to Permissions, Walker BFYR, 175 Fifth Avenue, New York, New York 10010

Library of Congress Cataloging-in-Publication Data
available upon request
ISBN 978-0-8027-3432-7 (hardcover) • ISBN 978-0-8027-3433-4 (reinforced)

Art created with watercolor and ink
Typeset in Old Claude

Printed in China by Hung Hing Printing (China) Co., Ltd., Shenzhen, Guangdong
2 4 6 8 10 9 7 5 3 1 (hardcover)
2 4 6 8 10 9 7 5 3 1 (reinforced)

For Frank S. Barker -
the original party animal -
with lots of love

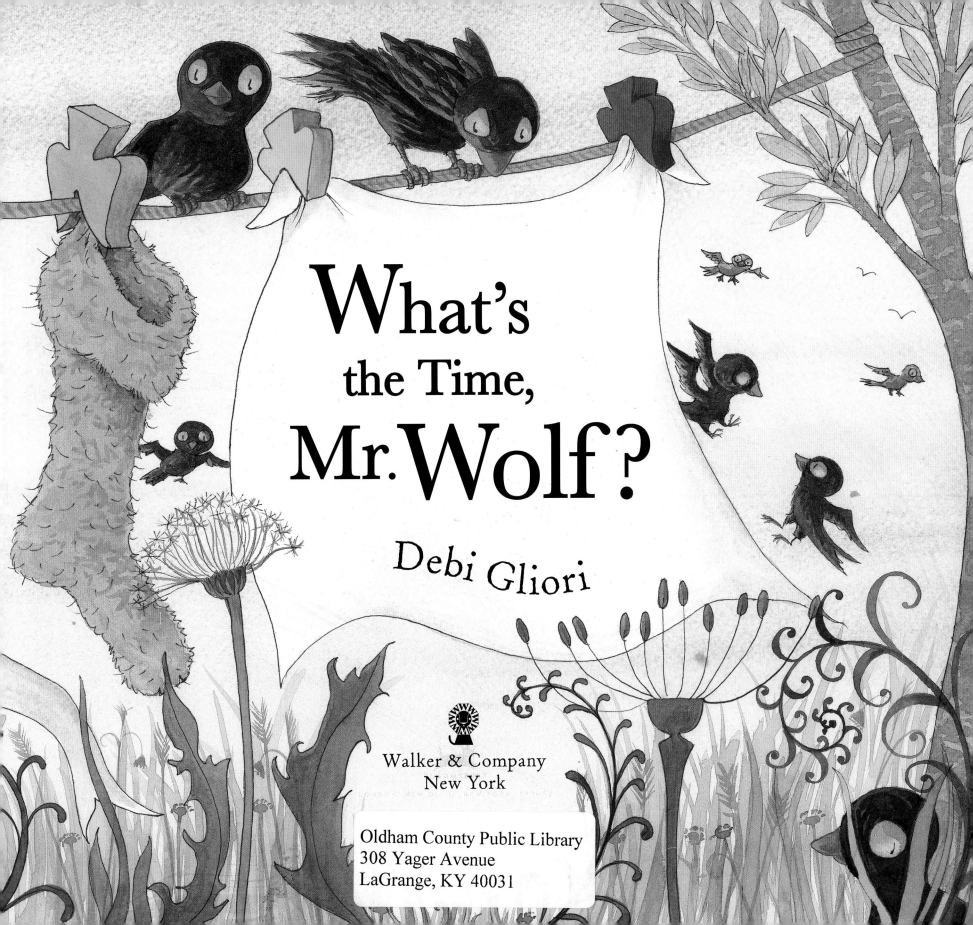

What's the Time, Mr.Wolf?

Debi Gliori

Walker & Company
New York

It is **seven** o'clock in the morning.
Mr. Wolf is woken up on his birthday by four and twenty blackbirds.

"What's the time, Mr. Wolf?" they tweet.
"It's time for blackbird pie," yawns Mr. Wolf.

It is **eight** o'clock in the morning. All of Mr. Wolf's neighbors slam their doors on their way to work.

BANG!

goes the door
of the stone house.

CRASH!
goes the door of the
wooden house.

THUD!
goes the door of the straw house.

"What's the time, Mr. Wolf?"
giggle the three little pigs.
"It's time for bacon sandwiches,"
mutters Mr. Wolf.

It is **nine** o'clock in the morning.

Here comes the girl in the little red hood, bringing the mail.

About time,
thinks Mr. Wolf,
running to the door.

But there is nothing for Mr. Wolf—not so much
as a card on his special day!
Poor Mr. Wolf.

It is **ten** o'clock in the morning.
Mr. Wolf is trimming the hairs on his
chinny-chin-chin when his phone rings.

Mr. Wolf hears a **snort**, then an **oink**, and a **giggle**.

Finally a voice squeals,
"What's the TIME, Mr. Wolf?"
"Not you three again," groans Mr. Wolf.
"It's time you little pigs bought a watch. Good-bye."
And he puts the phone down.

It is **eleven** o'clock in the morning.

Mr. Wolf's tummy gives a loud rumble.
What's the time, Mr. Wolf? he wonders.
Time for a snack?

But when he goes to his cupboard,
it is bare—even his dish has
run off with his spoon!

It is **twelve** o'clock.
Noon.
Time to go shopping,
thinks Mr. Wolf.

He is halfway to the store
when it starts to rain.
Time I bought an umbrella,
thinks Mr. Wolf.

It is
one o'clock
in the afternoon.

BONGGGG!

There's a mouse
running up
Mr. Wolf's clock.

"What's the time,
Mr. Wolf?" squeaks
the mouse.
But Mr. Wolf
doesn't answer.
Mr. Wolf is out.

It is **two** o'clock in the afternoon.
Mr. Wolf is at the bakery.

"What's the hurry, Mr. Wolf?" asks the baker man.

"I'm baking your cake as fast as I can,
patting and prodding and filling with jam,
bake for an hour then remove from the pan."

It is **three** o'clock
in the afternoon.

Mr. Wolf is tired and very, very hungry.
He is heading home when . . .

ZOOOOOOM! WHOOOOOOSH!

A crowd rushes past.

"No time to stop, Mr. Wolf," they gasp.
"We're already late."

It is **four** o'clock in the afternoon.
Mr. Wolf takes the shortcut home.
It is cool and shady under the trees.

"Time for a nap," says Mr. Wolf.

HEY DIDDLE-EE
DIDDLE-EE DIDDLE-EE
YOWWWL!

Mr. Wolf's eyes spring open.
There is a cat playing the fiddle.
"**Five** o'clock. Time to wake up,
Mr. Wolf," the cat says.
"Shall I play some more lovely
tunes on my fiddle?"

Mr. Wolf shudders.
"Good grief!" he says.
"Is that the time?
So sorry, must be going."
And he runs away
as fast as he can.

It is **six** o'clock.

BONG, goes Mr. Wolf's clock.

BONGGG! BONGGG!
BONGGG! BONGGG!
BONGGG!

"SSHHHhhhh!"

say Mr. Wolf's friends.

Mr. Wolf is nearly home. He climbs the step, lifts the latch, opens his door, and . . .

"Surprise! Happy birthday, Mr. Wolf!"

It's PARTY time!

And later. Much later.
All of Mr. Wolf's friends have gone home.

Mr. Wolf is brushing his teeth.

Mr. Wolf is pulling up the quilt.

"What's the time, Mr. Wolf?"
ask the stars.
But Mr. Wolf doesn't reply,
because Mr. Wolf is fast asleep.

It is BEDtime.